WEAVE THE DARK, WEAVE THE LIGHT

ANNA ZABO

ABOUT WEAVE THE DARK, WEAVE THE LIGHT

Fire witch Ari Zydik has always had a tenuous connection with their magic, and opening themself up to the whims of the universe on Samhain, desperate for a connection to *anything* hasn't helped. A chance run-in with a stranger while ice skating leads to a tenuous relationship with Jonathan Aster, an immortal and powerful being—one Ari feels compelled to conquer and dominate. But as Midwinter looms, can Ari tame the fire of an ancient star?

Representation: nonbinary gender, aromantic, pansexuality

Content note: Contains consensual kink, including pain play and on-page sex.

THE WAXING MOON hung high above Pittsburgh, bright and silver, illuminating nearby clouds crossing the night sky. Ari added their own ephemeral puff to PPG Plaza's chilly air. They'd already paid the fee and had a wristband to get onto the ice rink. All that was left was to lace their skates.

Had Theo and Bess joined Ari, no doubt they'd tease them for being a fire witch on ice. That was bullshit. Opposite elements attracted each other, and Ari enjoyed the chaos invoked between the two. They loved ice skating and swimming. The darkness of night. All the things they shouldn't. Rebellion was as close to Ari as the amber they wore against their skin and the citrine in the pocket of their red wool coat.

Colored lights from the spires of the glass castle surrounding the plaza cast a rainbow on the skaters. A lit tree in the center of the rink glittered, and upbeat Christmas tunes thrummed in the air, despite it being mid-November.

Ari glanced up, but between the lights and the bright moon, no stars hung in the sky—at least none they could see.

The stars watched, though. They always did, regardless of the moon or the lights or the season.

That knowledge was as frosty as the breath in Ari's lungs as they hit the ice, shaking away the thought. The night felt perilous, like the edge of a cliff.

Unfortunately, the surface of the rink was utter *crap*, full of snow, nicks, and gouges. They'd expected nothing less. Even with resurfacing, the small rink became scraped up minutes after the Zamboni chugged back into its lair.

Didn't matter. As long as they kept moving and tried nothing fancy, their skates would take them where they wanted—around and around until all that existed was the tinny music, the scrape of blades, and the fire Ari'd come to collect. Oh, their element was with them, long ribbons of fiery red, orange, and blue, but the heart in their magic was missing. The *passion*.

Ari hadn't felt whole since Samhain. They'd opened themself that day, and chaos had entered. Loneliness. Lack of desire. Which was apropos, in a way. They'd always had a tenuous connection to their magic and their element, and no one could explain why Ari's magic stuttered and fizzled even when they filled themself with as much fire as they could manage.

Bess had chided them—gently. "If you choose a path..."

They *had*. But no one else in their circle believed chaos was a proper path.

Tonight, to get away, Ari'd donned brilliant gold tights under their long black skirt, wrapped themself in a retro Joy Division sweatshirt, taken their skates, and slipped away from the apartment they shared with Theo.

There was magic in the laughter here, in the delighted shrieks of kids and the embarrassed, happy yelps of teens clinging to the walls of the rink. Power lurked in the grins of those who could spin, skate backward, and weave through the crowd.

Life. Delight. Happiness. Ari wrapped that warmth into their soul, a little spell to carry their hope through winter. Something to warm their heart when everything else was emptiness tinged with frustration.

Fire and water could be many things; the ice beneath their blades was proof enough of that. But fiery rage and anger weren't what Ari needed to chase away the void that had formed in their soul. Little spells worked—mostly. Larger spells fell flat. Life grated and itched. Ari found themself alone in a circle full of friends and an office full of coworkers.

Bess had told them to be specific with their spell, and they'd *tried*. They wanted a connection. Something less ephemeral than the occasional hookup. They had their friends and their job, but neither of those warmed their soul.

So much for opening themself up to the universe. The void between the stars had poured right in.

In front of Ari, another skater wobbled and fell. They leapt over tangled legs. Landing, however, sent Ari careering out of control until a gloved hand settled on their arm and a hard body steadied theirs.

"Careful." Amusement filled that voice. Power and danger.

Every piece of Ari's magic turned toward the stranger who'd caught them. Elemental energy clashed and wove around them—Ari's fire and something deadlier, tempting, and powerful.

The stranger was tall. A black knit hat covered light hair, and black leather gloves rested against Ari's coat. Inhumanly blue eyes caught theirs. A midnight peacoat was paired with a bright white scarf that glittered like diamonds. Those features could have been masculine, or not. There was something otherworldly, something terrifying and wonderful about that face. Light and cold. Darkness. Eternity.

Ari blinked, but the effect didn't vanish. "Thanks."

"Nice jump." Whoever they were let go. Still, Ari felt the pull of the other's magic, like gravity.

Passion bloomed in Ari's bones, the first they'd felt in months. The need to touch, taste, and share was almost painful in intensity.

The skater glided away and was lost in the crowd before Ari could voice a second thanks.

Shit.

Ari skated after them.

Despite the tiny size of the rink, Ari couldn't spot the person who'd caught them. There were black knit caps and leather gloves galore on tall strangers, but none wore a scarf full of light or had eyes as old as the universe.

Ari shivered. Not from cold—that never touched them —nor from fear, but from nearly extinct fervor sparking to life. This was intrigue and danger. Theo would've said to be careful. Bess would've cautioned against having anything to do with that particular stranger.

But Ari had a heart of knives and a soul of fire. Of course they'd follow.

A few more loops gave Ari time to settle, to whisper a charm, to trace symbols in their mind, and to collect wisps of fire. Then they stepped off the frozen water, thanked it for its presence and time, took their skates off, hoisted the carrying bag on their shoulder, and headed toward the Point.

In theory, Point State Park closed at sunset, but it was

also a pathway, part of the city, and this time of year, it was lit with LED trees and giant snowflakes on poles. Part of an old star fort was marked by a zigzagging path across a lawn. Ari walked under the bridge that sped an interstate over land, then water. Nature lurked beyond. Trees and shrubs. Native plants. A piece of wild at the edge of a city, bound by water.

Dried leaves scratched across concrete walkways, blown into tree beds. Some animal rustled in the underbrush. Ari strode past a tree made of lights strung like a maypole, made their way around the silent and drained water fountain, and came to a stop. They stared at the confluence of the rivers, their skates at their feet.

So much water. But fire too, in the passing trains across the river, in car engines on the interstate, and in boats slipping through the rivers.

Ari found their memory, the fine cord of emotion, that odd element, and used it to will the stranger back to them.

"Youth," that same voice said from behind, "is bold and reckless."

Ari's heart stuttered. "But you came." They turned enough to catch the brightness of the scarf. "And I'm not *that* young."

"I came." Agreement, and amusement, as well. The stranger stepped next to Ari, and cold fire curled around Ari's legs. "And you *are* that young if you're summoning *me*, little fire witch."

This time, Ari turned to regard the stranger's profile in the dim light. The hair that peeked out from their winter hat was as gray as the moon, and their scarf glittered like nothing had a right to do. Something magical dwelt inside this being. A flame that wouldn't burn—it would cause you not to exist.

Too much power swam inside and around them, an element Ari didn't understand but *tasted*. They should have been terrified. Instead, they craved the knowledge in those eyes and that skin under their fingers.

Ari swallowed. "You're not human."

"You knew I wasn't human the moment I touched you."

Ari had, but this wasn't any elemental being they'd heard about, that was for certain. Not fae, nor phoenix—the fire was the wrong type for that. Chilling white-blue, rather than blazing red, violet, and yellow. "What do I call you?" they murmured.

Those eyes locked on theirs. "My name's Jonathan Aster."

Aster like the bright flowers of late summer, the last color before the frost. "Pronoun?"

A twitch in Jonathan's lips. "*He* feels the most correct at the moment."

Ari filed away that tidbit and gazed out at the black water of the rivers that reflected the bright lights from the shores, the bridges, and the hills. They kept their name behind their lips.

Jonathan laughed. "It's only polite to gift me your name, seeing as you have mine."

Ari bristled and watched silver clouds slide across the sky. "It's Ari Zydik. And they."

Jonathan nodded. "Yes." As if it were an affirmation, as if he'd known their name already, as if he'd always known Ari.

What are *you?* This question remained on their tongue, though barely.

"What spells will you cast when you get home?" Jonathan slipped closer to the river, then turned, blocking the view. Ari had to study his face. "What will you make from the sparks you collected?"

"Is that any of your business?" Ari snapped.

A chuckle was the reply.

Jonathan was stunning in a delicate way. Strong lines. High cheekbones. Teeth as white as his scarf. His skin was darker than Ari's pale complexion. Even in the moonlight, the golden hue was evident. Sun-touched, but that still didn't seem like a fitting description.

Not an angel. Not a demon. Ari'd never met either, but Jonathan's energy was wrong for what had been described in the books they'd read. He was light *and* dark. There was a sense of eternity, but not timelessness. "You're old."

"Very." He stalked forward. "Very old."

"But you'll die." A sliver of space separated them. Ari watched blue eyes dance like the heart of the hottest flame.

"Eventually. But not for a long time." Soft words, a thin stream of smoke in the night air.

Energy whipped around Ari. They snatched it and drew it closer, devouring it.

Jonathan lifted his hand—but not in aggression. "You should ask before you take." His leather-clad fingers hovered near Ari's shoulder. "May I?"

They nodded, unsure of what Jonathan was asking, but so very sure they wanted whatever was being offered.

His palm cupped Ari's shoulder, and elemental energy slammed into them. Not fire—no, nothing so simple. This was a lick of lightning or the arc of a transformer, but colder. The depth of space.

The heart of the universe throbbed in Jonathan, a distant bell reverberating through the bones of the earth and the moon. Ari sucked the energy into their soul, wrapping themself around the wild, *untamable* joy.

Jonathan's lips parted in a feral parody of a smile. "Oh, little witch, you are something different."

Ari placed their hand on Jonathan's midnight peacoat and slipped two fingers between the buttons. "I'm hardly little." Hardly young or inexperienced. What would it be like to have this man under them? Bound? What would his skin taste like under lips and tongue? To linger in bed and talk about the mysteries of the universe?

Jonathan's laugh, sharp and biting, clouded the air. "Dangerous."

"You or me?"

"Me. You're merely reckless."

"Am I?" Ari pushed their fingers further into the coat, stroking the warm fabric that lay over muscle and bone.

"You have no idea what you're playing with." He removed his hand and took a step back, out of reach.

Ari brushed their thumb against their lips, tasting lingering warmth. "Not fire. You're not that."

"Certainly not *that*." Jonathan's scarf glittered in the moonlight, as did his eyes.

The latter blazed for a second, and Ari sucked in a breath, feeling that strange, cold brightness twine and burn within them. Ancient. Older than the world. "Starlight." The word fell from their lips. Of *course*. Aster. Star.

The playfulness on Jonathan's lips fell away.

"Plasma, then." Something Ari shouldn't have been able to draw or keep or even touch. And yet, they felt the strands inside them, as much as they could hold.

Reckless? Maybe. Dangerous? Most certainly. Even if Jonathan hadn't realized that.

"I should add brave to your list of descriptors," he murmured.

Ari stepped forward and touched the buttons of Jonathan's coat. "Why are you here?"

"Some secrets you have to earn, Ari."

They stood together for silent moments. Curiosity warred with frustration and slipped into lust. What would it be like to fuck a star? *This* star? To strip Jonathan of his clothes, tie him down, and take him apart? To verbally spar with him for hours? To be known physically and mentally by something so powerful? "And how does one earn your secrets, Jonathan?"

He unlooped the scarf from around his neck and draped it around Ari's, holding on to the ends. "Weave me a spell."

The fabric was shockingly warm against Ari's skin, or maybe that was their blush rising. Spells for another required a connection that didn't exist yet between them and Jonathan. Ari breathed out fear and drew in strength. "What sort of spell? Protection? Empowerment? Love?"

Jonathan tugged the scarf before letting the ends go. The motion brought Ari closer. "Your choice, fire witch." He paused. "Though I don't think anyone can spell someone into love."

"It's an alignment of intent. I can *help* with that, in the case of love. But if one party isn't interested..." They shrugged, dug into their pocket for the citrine they always carried, and handed it to Jonathan. Once again, when they touched, energy sparked. Ari pulled more into them.

"All magic is intent." Jonathan closed his fingers around the citrine before bringing it to his lips and kissing the stone. "It'll be interesting to see what you do with yours."

Ari wanted that mouth open in surprise and ecstasy, wanted to see Jonathan gasping in need. They wanted to know Jonathan—and wanted to be known in return.

"I had no idea humans could channel plasma. It's not an element anyone talks about."

"You, I believe, can do whatever you want." Jonathan tucked the stone into the pocket of his coat. "It might be a human trait, but I suspect that's peculiar to you." His smile was knife sharp. "I suppose we'll see."

"We'll meet again?" Those words were a blade pressed to Ari's throat, all thrill and adrenaline. They lifted their chin. Another chance to uncover Jonathan and unfold themself.

Maybe he understood, because he whispered into Ari's ear, "Most certainly."

"Good." Jonathan's neck was right there. If they turned, they could press their lips to Jonathan's skin. "I want to taste you."

This close, his laugh was like the rumble of distant thunder. "It's written into your every move."

Jonathan smelled of winter, rose, and the press of thorns. "I don't know anything about you." And he knew nothing of them. Oh, but they wanted that. Wanted to turn Jonathan inside out. Wanted to inhale his element as if it were air.

"You have my name, and you know what I am. The rest that you long for? You can find out."

"At what price?" There was always one with beings like this.

"I've told you." Johnathan straightened, but remained a breath apart. "Though I should ask you. What do you want, Ari Zydik? What price must I pay to know *you*?"

I don't know. But it was the word "control" that slipped from their lips. Both were true.

Jonathan's eyes glittered like the lights on the river. "That's quite the price."

Their laugh scratched across the empty park. "I know." Too much to ask.

A breeze teased the edges of Jonathan's hair, and he was as still and heavy as the hours before dawn. Ari held their breath.

Finally, Jonathan's lips curled up. "Take your taste," he murmured. "I'll consider your price."

They pressed their lips to Jonathan's neck, licking the skin there, and tasted mint and peril.

In the next moment, Jonathan closed his gloved hand around Ari's throat. Not hard, and not for long. Then he was walking around the silent, yawing fountain. "Enjoy the rest of your evening, Ari."

They could've followed, but heat rooted Ari to the ground. They watched Jonathan, who wasn't human at all, climb a set of stairs, walk past the Christmas tree, and across the moonlit lawn until he vanished.

Even then, Jonathan burned bright in Ari's mind and soul. They stood for a time, then collected their skate bag and trudged from the park, full of energy, lust, and trepidation.

It was a very long bus ride home.

2

MORNING CAME WAY the fuck too early, pulling Ari from dreams of lips, light, and thrusting. Their phone chirped with birdsongs and soft music, and it took three tries to grab the damn thing and shut it off. They stared at slivers of morning stretched across the ceiling, still achingly hard, their heart beating against their ribs and the phantom taste of Jonathan lingering in their mouth.

What remained of the dream drifted away faster than they could pull it back. Only the hollow ache in their soul, the memory of Jonathan, and their stiff dick remained. They'd never been good at lucid dreaming nor at remembering their dreams.

"There's too much fire in you," Chole had said. She wove air and earth and practically lived in her dreams. The spells she'd given Ari hadn't helped. Strange that their inability would stem from fire, since Matty wove fire, but he'd never had issues remembering his dreams. None of their circle did, but Ari.

Another reminder of how, even in the middle of their

circle, they were alone. "I want to belong," they'd told Theo before Samhain, when they'd both been working on their spells.

Theo had peered back if they'd grown three heads. "But you do."

They'd not mentioned that again, to anyone.

Last night, they'd tasted a star.

Fuck. Ari struggled out of their heavy nest of blankets. They still hummed with the energy they'd sipped from Jonathan, even after casting last night. Scattered about were sigils drawn on pages and crystals holding fire and light. Still, Ari's blood burned and sparked, and Jonathan's strange blue eyes, pale hair, and golden skin lingered in their thoughts. His scent clung to their nostrils.

Weave me a spell.

Wasn't so simple. When they'd returned home, they'd lit incense, cleared the space, and focused on setting down spell after spell while Jonathan's element was fresh inside them. Protection. Empowerment. One for sparking creativity. Even a love potion. Everything had turned flat, as spells had before. Yes, there was energy in the sigils and crystals but not *intent*, not power. The spells would never work as they should. Ari'd have to bleed the magic out of them later.

They had no idea what Jonathan wanted. Hell, they weren't sure what they wanted.

A connection. Understanding.

Ari shook away those thoughts. Sex and control were ideas they could wrap their mind around. Lust was an old friend. Everything else sounded perilously close to something they had no framework for, no way to navigate.

Didn't help that they'd tripped over Theo's black sneakers and Bess's purple heels last night, and now dreaded leaving their room. Ari liked Bess a lot—she'd encouraged needed grounding in their circle. Bess had focused the group and brought order.

They chafed at order, though. Some structure was fine, but on their own terms, not enforced by others. Bess tended to mother Ari, even though they were all about the same age and had been studying magic for similar amounts of time.

Ari darted into the bathroom and showered, then dove back into their room to change, hoping they'd escape before either Bess or Theo woke up. No such luck. Bess lingered in the bedroom doorway, wrapped in a robe, her long braids stark black lines against red silk.

Of course she noticed Jonathan's scarf in Ari's hand, shimmering like starlight even as morning sun streamed through the hallway window.

"Where'd you get that, baby doll?" Her gaze flicked from the scarf and pinned Ari with a *look*.

"Not your baby doll," Ari drawled before heading to the living room. "And a guy gave it to me last night."

"That's no ordinary scarf, love." Bess followed.

"No shit." Ari drew the scarf around their neck and pulled on their coat. They let the *love* go. It was better than *doll* any day.

Bess planted a hand on her hip. "So, what did you give this *guy* in return for that, hmm?" The way her tone changed, Ari knew she was asking: *who did you fuck for that scarf?*

Ari laughed. Yeah, they wanted Jonathan, wanted to push him down and have their every way with him. But sex for a scarf, even one wrapped in magic? Please.

Not on the first night, anyway.

"I gave him a piece of citrine." They paused. "And the

promise of a spell." They'd started a dance with Jonathan that Ari didn't understand, but felt the rhythm nonetheless.

Bess stepped closer. "Oh, Ari." There was worry in her voice. Honest, actual worry. "What *kind* of spell?"

"Look, I gotta get to work. I don't have time to play twenty questions." Maybe they were as reckless as Jonathan said.

"What, spell, *what?*" Theo echoed sleepily as he stepped into the living room. His eyes locked onto Ari, and he straightened, all weariness vanishing. "Whoa, Ari." Theo's brown eyes were wide and fearful. "That's not fire in you. What the *fuck?*"

That was a drawback to living with Theo—he was an earth witch who could work water as well, but unlike Ari, Theo saw more than just his own elements—he saw them *all*, including Jonathan's, it seemed. *Definitely* time to leave. "It's nothing. It's *fine*. I'm fine. I'm gonna be late." Ari grabbed their backpack and ran out of the apartment.

They took the stairs rather than wait for the elevator. They couldn't handle the look in Theo's eyes, or the one in Bess's.

They both cared about Ari—that was mutual—but Ari didn't know if the *family* thing worked. They'd never be able to convince their circle that Jonathan wasn't dangerous, especially since Jonathan was *terrifying*. Might as well be a demon, but he *wasn't*. He was a deep part of existence, an ancient spark of energy.

Weave me a spell.

Why would a star need a witch's spell? And how the hell was Ari going to create one when they didn't know what Jonathan needed?

Despite the mention of love spells, they were sure romance wasn't what Jonathan wanted. And besides, Ari didn't love easily. Sex was fun and uncomplicated. Friendships were foundational. Romantic love was...*messy*. Ari had enough chaos in their life. Sex, though...that might be a singular focus they needed in order to weave magic. Granted, with their kinks, that particular avenue involved tying Jonathan up, and they suspected the answer to the price they'd set would be no.

Ari slung their bag onto their back. The walk and wait at the bus stop wasn't long, and no one seemed to notice anything more odd about Ari than normal. They were wearing black tights and a long navy skirt, a crisp white button-down, and a brilliant red bow tie that peeked from their coat. Combat boots rounded out the outfit. There might be snow later, and no way were they risking good shoes to crap weather. Besides, they liked the boots—all that black leather.

Squirrel Hill was pretty laid-back, but they'd probably get some looks later in the commute, especially since they'd skipped shaving. Whatever. They knew who they were.

When the bus came, Ari snagged a window seat.

Businesses, houses, and streets blurred past. Ari pulled Jonathan's scarf tighter around their neck, catching the faint smell of him—peppermint and smoke. *Impossible*. Still, Ari buried their nose in the fabric.

They didn't pay attention to the other passengers until someone sat next to them and a rush of cold fire wrapped around their limbs. Ari whipped their gaze from the window and found Jonathan's razor smile. "Hello, Ari."

"How—" Ari snapped their mouth shut and swallowed. Not the smartest question. They had Jonathan's scarf and he had Ari's citrine. "I have work today."

Without his hat, his hair was silver-gray. His skin was warm, in tone and touch, when he patted Ari's thigh with an ungloved hand. "I know. But you've been in my thoughts and in my head, and I was curious to see you."

"Curious to see me," Ari repeated. They drank in the sight of Jonathan and the warmth of his body. "You could've gotten my number, you know. Texted. Asked me out for coffee."

Jonathan—the fucking elemental star—looked at his hands. "Yes. But your cell number's not a piece of you." He drew the citrine from his coat pocket and turned it over in his fingers. "This is."

Ari curled their hands into the scarf, wishing they were curled in Jonathan's hair. "But you can't use that to ask me out for coffee."

Jonathan focused entirely on Ari. "It's not coffee I want."

Desire ripped through Ari. They grasped the scarf, the licks of element coming off of Jonathan, and pulled both close to themself.

Jonathan's eyes flickered, as if in pleasure. "Maybe you *are* dangerous, little witch."

"Oh, I am." Sitting next to Jonathan chased away the worries and the doubts of the morning. This felt *right*. They'd ponder *why* later. "There's a price for more." Despite being wicked and honed, Ari had also been hot and sharp most of their life.

"So you've named." Thoughtfulness in the set of his mouth. "Control is a heady thing, and I'm your equal, Ari."

Equal. Ari turned that unfathomable piece of knowledge over in their head, and wanted to dispute it, but Jonathan spoke it as fact. "Wouldn't be all the time," they said. "Just—in certain situations."

A slow nod. "Not over coffee, I expect."

Ari laughed. Couldn't help it. They *liked* Jonathan, in

that moment. Trepidation clung to Ari—Jonathan wasn't human and he wore power like a second skin—but he was also intriguing and smiled like sunlight.

"I'll pay your price," he said, just like that.

Ari exhaled, and yes, control took their mind into the clouds. There were so many ways this could go wrong. They leaned close to his beautiful face and whispered, "My stop is coming up, so here's what's going to happen." They pressed a hand over the citrine, palm touching Jonathan's where it could. "You're going to find me after work, treat me to a lovely dinner like the gentleman you are; then I'm going to take you home, tie you up, and fuck you like the monster I am."

Jonathan's feral smile returned, and he moved his lips close to Ari's. "Reckless."

"You can say no." They wanted to lean in and kiss him, but their stop was next.

"You know I won't," Jonathan said. "Your offer is interesting."

Ari couldn't help a grin of their own. They reached back and hit the strip to signal the bus stop. "It's not an offer, Jonathan."

"Ah." If anything, his smile deepened.

They bumped his legs. "Time for me to go."

He nodded and tucked the citrine back in his pocket before standing. Ari slid into the aisle, but not before Jonathan brushed a hand down Ari's back. "I want my spell, though."

"You'll get it. I don't break promises." They caught Jonathan's hand and squeezed. "Any of them." They let go and headed to the front of the bus. Didn't look back when they stepped off. Jonathan might be there—or might not. They had no idea how this elemental existed in the world, except that, somehow, Jonathan was real and solid to Ari.

So, they were going to do exactly what they said they would. Maybe more time with Jonathan would unlock the spell he was so desperate for Ari to weave.

3

JUST AFTER FIVE, Ari walked out of the office. They hadn't expected Jonathan to be waiting in the lobby. Same peacoat, same pale hair, golden skin, and tantalizing smile. He turned the citrine over in his hand, and his bright blue eyes burned straight through Ari.

The pack of coworkers they'd left with broke apart, with choruses of "Good night" and "See you Monday." Ari murmured some kind of response, their being entirely focused on Jonathan.

"Ari." He said their name like a prayer, as if there was no one else in the lobby. He held out his arm, as if they were on a *date*. "Shall we?"

"This isn't a romance, Jonathan." Still, they took his arm.

"Oh, I'm aware." Together they pushed through the doors into the evening.

"What do you think this is?"

Jonathan guided them through the streets of Pittsburgh, the air blustery, dry, and harsh, hinting at the winter to come. "A beginning."

They shook their head. That had been last night. They had prices and promises between them. "We've already started."

That sharp smile again. "A continuation, then. A discovery." He paused at the door to Meat & Potatoes. "Does this qualify as a lovely dinner?"

Very much so. Ari'd managed to eat at the small restaurant once before, but that was only because there'd been an opening at the bar. "If they can seat us."

They stood under the portico of Theater Square, out of the lash of wind that cut down Penn Avenue. "Oh, we have a reservation." And fuck if Jonathan's grin didn't turn Ari inside out with the need to kiss him into submission. He propped opened the door for Ari.

They entered and didn't ask how Jonathan had managed a near-impossible feat on a morning's notice. A discovery, indeed. There was so much Ari wanted to understand. So much they feared to ask, both of Jonathan and for themself.

Jonathan followed, and as he'd assured, there was a reservation for two under his name. They settled into their table.

Ari pulled a little of Jonathan's element and wove it into a simple spell, lessening the chance of being overheard. Maybe it was possessive of them, but they didn't want to share this night with anyone else. Ari skimmed the menu, but their mind kept wandering to unasked questions. "Do you exist in this world?"

Jonathan stilled, the menu motionless in his hands. "We're here, Ari. Right now. This isn't a dream."

Of course it wasn't a dream. "That's not what I'm asking." Ari tore their gaze from Jonathan and read the menu again. "When I'm not here, what do you do? Where do you go?"

Jonathan laid his menu down. "Ah. I understand. Yes, I exist in this world and time. When I'm not with you, I'm still here. People see me." He folded his hands on top of the menu and curved his mouth into a smile. "As to what I do, I own a used bookstore."

"Isn't that a little cliché?"

Ari was growing fond of Jonathan's laugh. "Perhaps, but people like me tend to gravitate toward antique items. Or collections. Or"—he waved a hand—"oddities."

Information twined in Ari's skull. "Are you telling me bookstores and antique shops are all run by magical beings?"

"Not all, surely." His smile didn't diminish.

"I—"

Before they could get their question out, the waiter arrived to take their order. Ari had no idea what they wanted, but one good thing about this place was that they couldn't go wrong with anything on the menu. Ari stabbed at a random dish and rattled the name off.

"I'll have the same." Jonathan handed his menu over, then tilted his head. "Wine?"

"Not tonight." They wanted a clear head, especially for later. "Water is fine for us."

The waiter took the menus, then retreated, leaving Ari caught by the intense desire to put the proud, powerful man before them on his knees. "Why me?"

"You called *me*, Ari. Not the other way around."

"You found me at the rink."

"You were looking for me."

"I was looking—" They'd been looking for passion. For the spark that had been missing from their life. Searching to understand their magic, for a sense of belonging. "But you've been in Pittsburgh for years, I suspect."

"Yes." He dropped his hands to his lap. "As have you."

"Since college." They'd gotten their degree, then stayed, even though they could have found a job elsewhere. Something about this town, its hills, rivers, and bridges had wormed its way into Ari's soul. "I felt compelled to stay."

"Life is strange and magical."

Every amazing moment in Ari's life had been. Even meeting Theo and Bess. Some moments had been fraught. Some dangerous. But always infused with magic and power. "What do you want with me?"

Jonathan lowered his gaze, his smile demure. If he'd planned to reply, it was lost as two glasses filled with water were set in front of them.

There was attraction, one neither of them could deny or ignore. Hell, Jonathan's element practically wrapped itself around Ari unbidden. They pulled and wove it in a way they'd never been able to with fire. Maybe *this* was what being a strong witch was like, this ability to tap into energy and use it—make it part of themselves.

They pondered while they waited for their meal, and then while reveling in the taste of their flat iron steak. The lull that fell between them wasn't uncomfortable, especially not when Ari shifted to nudge their leg against Jonathan's.

"I'm going to answer your question with one of my own," Jonathan said. "Why do you want me, Ari?"

So many reasons. The most obvious being simple lust for a stunningly beautiful person. The need to tame someone powerful. However, neither of those hit the core of the truth. "Because I want to understand what you are." Ari set down their fork. "Will you answer my original question?"

He sobered into a seriousness that twisted Ari's bones and set every part of them alight. "What I want with you is *you*. Because you hunt answers, Ari Zydik. Beyond the need to control, aside from the myriad ways our bodies could come together. You seek more from me alongside those, and that's rare. That's a taste *I* want."

"Others have had you."

A shrug. "I *am* old." The grin returned. "*You* are not anyone else, though. I want you, in whatever way you wish to have me."

"Good." Very good. That gave them something to focus on other than the zing of awareness and yearning in their marrow. Lust was knowable, something they could temper and work.

Jonathan chuckled. "Would you like to hear about my rather normal life?"

Ari wanted to take Jonathan home, stretch him out, and see how much he could endure of Ari's flogger. But to know Jonathan was a desire that lay deep in Ari, more than sex or pain or pleasure. "Sure."

True to what Jonathan said, his life was mostly normal. His store carried a variety of books, and also specialized in antiquarian volumes he had a knack for finding. "I have good luck."

"Like finding me?"

Jonathan shook his head. "That was your doing, my sweet witch."

"Like managing reservations on a Friday night at a place that's usually booked out weeks in advance?"

That impish grin returned, and he sipped his water.

"The things I want to do to you," Ari murmured. The questions they needed to ask, the answers they wanted to find.

"Yes. Please."

Weave me a spell. Those words from last night hung like a challenge in their mind, sounded like the crack of a whip and the murmur of candleflame. Ari flagged down the waiter to ask for the check. Once their dishes had been cleared and Jonathan had paid, they strolled into the night. The air was sharp and crisp, and the moonlight turned Jonathan's hair silver.

Something in Ari's chest unwound. They'd called this man, this being to them. Jonathan was a sudden calm in the middle of the storm that had been Ari's life. "Does it bother you that I want to tie you up?"

"No." He peered at the sky as they walked, arm in arm, to Ari's bus stop. "Not at all. And you want to do far more than tie me up, Ari."

Much more. They pulled Jonathan to a halt. "May I kiss you?"

"Of course." Need lay in that confirmation.

Ari took the lapels of Jonathan's peacoat and pulled him to them. His lips were cool, but everything else burned when they deepened that kiss into something wanton and painful. A moan escaped Jonathan, and Ari drank the sound down. When they pulled back, Jonathan's expression was equal parts ravaged and wanting.

He licked his lips. "You should definitely take me home, tie me up, and fuck me."

This time, it was Ari who laughed, dark joy ringing into the night. He pulled Jonathan back into a walk, one quicker than before. If they were lucky, they'd catch the next bus. If not, Ari would spend the next half hour kissing Jonathan's lovely mouth.

Either option was acceptable.

THEY MADE it into Ari's apartment and to their room in a blur of touches, tastes, and motion, the pull between them finally overwhelming them both. Jonathan's energy exploded in Ari's mind and magic. They consumed Jonathan's mouth the same way they sucked down his element, folding both into their soul.

Jonathan tasted of the night and darkness and joy. Of a light Ari didn't understand and an energy they couldn't get enough of. Jonathan was wonder and danger. He felt like *home*.

They pushed Jonathan against the wall by their bedroom door, kicking the latter closed with their foot. "I need you naked. Now."

Beneath Jonathan's bronze skin lay a blush that darkened everything, from the look in those starlit eyes to the word that tumbled from his kiss-bruised lips. "Yes."

He made short work of undressing, peeling off clothing to reveal silken flesh stretched over muscle. The hair that dotted his chest and curled around his cock was the same pale gray Ari had caught under moonlight at the skating rink, beneath a furiously simple black cap.

He was magnificent and unworldly. Godlike. "Get on your knees."

Jonathan knelt, his gaze never leaving theirs. Energy whipped between them, lifting Ari's hair, rustling their skirt. It burned their veins. They wanted to devour every burst, then thrust it back into Jonathan. "Do you have a safeword?"

Jonathan blinked. "There's nothing you can do that will harm me."

Ari combed their fingers through Jonathan's hair, then

tightened their grip until Jonathan winced. "I don't want to harm you; I want to *hurt* you, but not beyond what you're willing to bear. If not for yourself, then have one for me so I know you consent." They pulled Jonathan's head back, until his proud throat was exposed, and his body taut against Ari's.

"Then Cygnus," he whispered. "Let it be Cygnus."

The swan. The constellation. When Ari let go, Jonathan gave a little groan. "You can be as rough as you'd like."

That was a dangerous thing to say. Ari hiked up their skirt and pulled down their tights. They stroked themself, watching Jonathan's hungry face. "Do you want me, Jonathan?" Their voice was rough and sharp, betraying desperation.

"Ari." His reply was a rumble. "You know I do."

Ari grasped Jonathan's chin and guided their cock into his willing, hot mouth. They both moaned, Jonathan's vibrating all around Ari. They thrust slowly at first, then with more force, their fingers twisted hard into Jonathan's hair.

His hands climbed Ari's legs.

"No. Behind your back, Jonathan. Surrender yourself to me."

That whimper was the most powerful sound Ari'd ever heard. The moment a being full of power and eternity yielded to Ari's will.

Energy shifted, twined, and flooded the room. Ari nearly came right there, thrusting deep into Jonathan's throat. Instead, they pulled out and stepped back. Both their breaths were gulps, and Ari's voice cracked as if they'd been the one on their knees. "Ever been cuffed and flogged, Jonathan?"

He shook his head. Behind those exquisite features, Ari spied excitement and fear. That only whetted their appetite. They pulled him to his feet and hauled him to their four-poster bed.

Yes, it was large. Yes, it occupied most of the room and had been hell to move. It also had hooks and rope hanging in perfect places, ready to be tied. "Stand here. Don't move."

"Yes, Ari." Jonathan's chest heaved.

Ari stripped their shirt on the way to their dresser and discarded their tights and shoes. They kept the skirt on. Took only a moment to find the cuffs and their favorite flogger before they returned to Jonathan. "Give me your wrists."

He obeyed sweetly, and Ari nearly groaned as they bucked the leather cuffs on. Lazy tendrils of Jonathan's element wrapped around Ari in return. "Don't get smart."

"Wouldn't dream of it." The snap in Jonathan's voice said otherwise.

They turned Jonathan around, then tied him to the bed, limbs stretched wide. Ari drew their hands down Jonathan's arms and back, then bit his shoulder, hard enough to garner them a gasp and a tremble. They reached around and stroked Jonathan's dick and bit a matching bruise into Jonathan's other shoulder.

"Please."

Ari nodded. "Soon."

Ari wasn't sure what Jonathan was begging for—pain, pleasure, or that spell. They dropped to their knees to cuff Jonathan's ankles, leaving Jonathan stretched between the pillars of Ari's bed, before nipping one of Jonathan's ass cheeks. He yanked on the ropes.

"Behave," they whispered against Jonathan's thigh.

"You don't want me to."

That was true. Ari wanted snark and mouth and all the power Jonathan could offer. They wanted to consume him, beat him, fuck him, and give him everything he wanted.

Weave me a spell.

A groan escaped Ari. They picked up their flogger and went to work, slowly. Gently, even. But as Jonathan twisted, shuttered, and moaned, they hit harder and faster. Under their blows, Jonathan's back reddened and welts appeared. Leather cut into golden flesh and bright red points blossomed.

Broken skin. Blood. Jonathan's energy streamed out of him with each moan, and Ari sucked it down as if they could hold the whole universe in their soul. With each stroke of the flogger, Jonathan cried out, raw and guttural. No way Theo and Bess didn't hear. Or their neighbors. Ari didn't care. They laid into Jonathan until they didn't think he could take much more—until Ari knew that *they* couldn't take more.

When they stopped, silence engulfed the room, disrupted by harsh breathing. Energy swarmed—so much power, Ari was drunk with it. Jonathan hung his head. All that held him from falling were the cuffs around his wrists.

Ari set the flogger on the bed and slid their hands up Jonathan's sides, his skin warm and damp with sweat. "You're exquisite, Jonathan. Beautiful."

"Thank you." His words were rough and full of tears. "Thank you for this."

Ari's emotions swirled like the energy in the room, looping and bobbing and tying themselves into knots. Their throat tightened too much to speak, so they kissed his back and ran teeth over the wounds they'd made, tasting sweat and blood. Ari stroked Jonathan as he shuddered and moaned, soaked in his essence, took their combined energy, and pushed it back into Jonathan's brightness. Then they unhooked the cuffs from the frame and lowered Jonathan to the bed, gathering his wrists at the small of his back. "I'm leaving your ankles cuffed."

"Yes, Ari."

"I'm going to fuck you, Jonathan. Like I want. Like I think you need." They leaned down over that prone body and pressed their cock into the cleft of Jonathan's ass with only the cloth of their skirt between. "Hard and deep, until I come inside you. Tell me I can."

"Yes." Jonathan squirmed, and the friction and the heat were perfect. "Good." His voice was stronger. "I want you. I need—"

Ari yanked Jonathan's hair and took his mouth in a sloppy brutal kiss that had him—had them both—trembling. When Ari broke away, they kissed Jonathan's cheek. "You taste divine. Your blood. Your tears. Your soul."

A faint smile graced his lips.

Ari pushed off and fetched the lube. Prepping Jonathan was a delight, from smacking his ass to sliding fingers into him while he moaned and panted and cursed.

"Oh, now you have a mouth." They hiked up their skirt and pressed the head of their cock against Jonathan's hole.

"You weren't teasing me when you were beating me. Now—"

Ari pushed inside. Whatever Jonathan had planned to say vanished into a soft, long cry of pleasure that echoed in Ari's chest.

As with flogging, Ari started slowly, giving them both time to adjust to the other before they picked up speed. Ari held Jonathan's wrists in one hand, and the nails of their other dug into his hip. Under them, Jonathan became a gasping, moaning mess. Ari pulled starlight from Jonathan, swallowed it, then pushed it back into him with every hard snap of their hips. Maybe they were both glowing. A little lost, a little dazed.

This was magic: Ari taking Jonathan and Jonathan opening himself for it. They were a witch, and Jonathan was their element—a living, breathing, embodiment of power.

Right now, that embodiment had welts on his back and was riding Ari's cock. "You really wanted this, didn't you?" A strange thought, especially when voiced. Jonathan could've had whomever he wanted, yet Ari was the one controlling his pliant, submissive body.

Something part laugh but mostly moan poured out of Jonathan. "Don't you dare stop."

Ari smacked his ass. Fucked him harder, pushed him closer, until the only sounds tumbling from Jonathan's smart mouth were deep cries.

Ari didn't stop. They relished Jonathan's release, cries turned to gasps, then whimpers. They let go of Jonathan's wrists, grabbed his hair, and yanked. "I'm not done with you yet."

"Good, please..." It was a breathless reply that stabbed into Ari.

Please.

Weave me a spell.

They had no idea what Jonathan wanted, but they gave him all they could—their body, the energy they'd collected, and every piece of pleasure and pain they could coax from both their bodies. On and on until Ari was shouting out their own release, burying themself inside Jonathan, and slamming more element than they should've been able to hold into the heart of the star underneath them.

Apparently, sex with Jonathan was like dying and being

reborn into a powerful creature. Even afterward, when Ari should have been spent and light with fatigue, they buzzed with awareness.

Jonathan, however, was a happy lump of well-fucked man. Ari freed his legs, cleaned him up, and coaxed him under the covers.

"Please say you're joining me," he murmured.

There was something sweet about that plaintive request. Ari kissed him on the cheek. "It's my bed. I'm gonna sleep in it." They stripped off their skirt. "Gotta clean me up too."

"Ah." A sleepy, happy sound.

No motion or lights lit the rest of the apartment, save the tiny night-light in the bathroom. If Theo and Bess were home, they'd gone to bed too. Ari had no idea what time it was, and didn't care. At all. They cleaned themself up, then returned to curl up with Jonathan.

They crawled into bed, looped their arms around him, and pulled him close. "I hope you enjoyed that."

"Oh, little witch, you have no idea."

Ari snorted. "Not so little."

Jonathan Aster—an actual damn star—*giggled*. "That's *very* true."

"Go to sleep, Jonathan."

He did. And after a long time spent listening to Jonathan breathe, wondering if the buzz still dancing inside them was permanent, Ari did, as well.

4

THE WEIGHT of Bess's and Theo's gazes was almost a physical presence as Ari moved around the kitchen. Before Ari'd ventured from their room, Jonathan, in a murmur that was all sleep and haze, had said he wouldn't mind some coffee. Apparently, elementals could have sex and kink hangovers just like anyone else. But his smile had been bright and his mouth pliant when Ari'd kissed him. They'd have fucked Jonathan awake, but they were nursing their own haze from the night before, and the tangled buzz mixed with their spinning mind meant conversation was a better plan than sex.

They wanted to understand what had happened and pick through the moments in peace. Spend time with Jonathan. Ask the questions flying around their head.

The *last* thing Ari wanted was to engage with Bess and Theo. Maybe later—but not now.

Ari broke the silence by grinding coffee beans. After they poured the grounds into the maker and started the pot, they turned around to face Theo and Bess.

Bess opened her mouth as if to speak, but flattened her

lips instead. She shook her head. Theo cleared his throat. "You—Ari, you brought an elemental—a fucking lightning elemental or something—home. He could've burned down the house!"

"I know what he is. And he wouldn't."

"You don't know that." Theo's tone took on the scolding quality Ari disliked.

"I do, though." They leaned against the counter, letting the edge bite into their hands. The discomfort cleared their head a little. Every nerve felt stretched and pinched. They wanted coffee and Jonathan; was that too much to ask?

Bess loosened her arms from across her chest. "We're concerned, that's all."

"You always are." The coffee pot gurgled and sputtered. Theo and Bess meant well, they truly *did*, but Ari was so damn tired of it. They poured two mugs of coffee and hefted them. "I'm fine. The house is fine. I'll talk to you later, okay?" They didn't wait for an answer.

Back in their room, Jonathan lounged in bed, seemingly fragile and indestructible, hair a disaster, torso lined with marks and shadowed bruises. His posture was almost demure, but his eyes were delighted flames. Ari handed him a mug, then settled on the bed next to him. "Theo thinks you're a lightning elemental and you're going to burn down the house."

Jonathan huffed a laugh before sipping his coffee.

"Are there lightning elementals?"

"First, define what you mean by elemental."

Ari gazed into their coffee. "Everyone says the fae are elementals. Water, air, earth."

"Fire?"

"You know there aren't fire fae." They gripped their mug tighter. "I never understood that. It makes no *sense*."

Then again, neither did Jonathan existing. The lack of knowledge, the confusion in Ari twisted like a knife in their gut.

Jonathan's soft touch pulled them out of their thoughts. "There are beings you might call lightning elementals, but they're nothing like me, or the fae, or anything you might also use that word to describe."

Maybe it was the aftermath of the night before, or the energy still swirling in the room, but Ari's emotions stretched and tumbled. Ari might be sharp and dangerous in their own way, but they were mortal and ignorant in so many others. "There's nothing about that in the books I've read. No one's ever told me about stars or lightning or why there are no damn fire fae." Ari hated the sound of their voice, tight and cracking, even as frustration tightened their lungs and stole breath. "Or what the hell I am." A mediocre fire witch who'd somehow called a star to them. That was as impossible as all the rest.

A clink of ceramic on wood, then Jonathan's arms were around Ari, drawing them back against his warm chest. "You're lovely, that's what you are."

Ari snorted. "If you're trying to woo me, that's going to fail."

"Is it?" They could almost feel Jonathan's smile against their skin.

They'd asked the universe for a connection, and Jonathan had appeared, bright and shining into their life. They wanted this to last and last.

Ari whispered the first dangerous question. "Will you teach me what I want to know?"

"There's a price." Jonathan's hot breath made Ari shiver.

"There always is." They drew Jonathan's arm up so they could lick and nip at a bruise they'd placed there last night.

Jonathan shuddered, and his voice dripped with the edge of a moan. "Everything goes two ways, Ari. Magic. Sex. Answers. Come home with me tonight."

Ari turned in Jonathan's arms so they could claim his mouth. Once they'd kissed Jonathan into a writhing mess, they answered, "I can do that."

His smile was a spell of its own. "Good."

THAT NIGHT, Ari packed a bag and rode the T with Jonathan to his South Hill's home. "Tomorrow," Jonathan said, "if you'd like, we can visit my shop."

"I still find strange that you have a shop. And a job. And a home." They ran their hand along his thigh. "All normal things."

He caught their hand and laced his fingers between theirs. "Even the fae exist in this world. Some are hidden, yes, but when you live for long enough you get—bored."

"Am I a cure for your *boredom*?" They raised an eyebrow.

Jonathan pressed the stop request strip. "Being alive is a cure for my boredom. You, my dear, are a wonderful, unexpected delight."

Jonathan's energy twined inside them, coiling like a snake. Ice and fire. So many questions Ari needed to ask, so much they wanted to know.

Jonathan stood. "This is my stop."

Together they made their way out of the train onto the platform. The night was cold and clear, with few stars peeking out from the moonlight sky. Ari's breath clouded the air as they peered into the night. "Can you see yourself up there? You're not in two places at the same time, are you?"

Jonathan glanced up. "When it's dark enough, yes. But I'm not in two places." He waved his free hand at the sky. "When you look at the stars, you're looking backward in time. This is now." He gestured to the street beyond the train platform. "I'm right here with you."

With them. That was terrifying. "This still isn't a romance."

"Does it need to be?" Jonathan hadn't unlaced his fingers from theirs.

Ari turned the question over in their mind as Jonathan led them into a residential area.

Another dangerous question slipped past their lips. "What do you want this to be?"

Jonathan slowed to a stop. Breath still smoked into the night, and Ari resisted slipping their hand into Jonathan's coat. There was light in his eyes, sparkling and gentle. Ari ached standing near him.

He brushed his fingers against their cheek. "You lead, Ari. I'll follow. Whatever you wish."

"So, I get to wish upon you?"

A dark smile. "You get to do many, *many* things upon me."

"Then we should go to your house, so I can do that." Lovely things. Wicked things. Things that would make Jonathan moan and scream. Magic things. They'd devour Jonathan's energy and thrust it back into him. Make him bleed.

Weave me a spell.

The streets were quiet but for the distant sound of cars and the deep thrum of gas furnaces cooling homes. Ari sensed the fire there, warm and inviting, even as Jonathan's cold flame tangled around their legs. "I called you."

"And I came."

"I should have called sooner."

A bright cloud of air came with Jonathan's laugh. "Perhaps. But we have time."

Did they? Jonathan had time. He could look into the past and see himself in the sky. Ari guessed Jonathan's future was as seemingly endless. But their life—that was another story. Though, right now, they were young and here *with* Jonathan.

A turn down a street, then half a block. "Here we are."

Jonathan's home wasn't big, but it was brick and light shown from the windows where the blinds hadn't been pulled down. The ubiquitous hum of heating rumbled from the house, a hint of fire seeping out.

Took only a moment for Jonathan to unlock the front door and usher Ari inside. The space was warm, both from the heated air and the rich wood that accented every room. "This is—cozy." They hadn't expected that.

"The house was built in the '40s," Jonathan said, "but it has lovely Art Deco touches from the '30s. Adds to the charm." There was pride in his voice as he took Ari's coat and the scarf he'd given them, and hung both in the closet. "Let me show you around."

Unlike the mad scramble into Ari's apartment, this was settled and quiet, though desire lurked deep in Ari's soul. The need to be naked again with Jonathan. To touch and tease and kiss and bite and scratch—and to cuddle.

Calm mixed with their growing passion.

Jonathan had book shelves filled to the brims. Artwork from simple to breathtaking. He also had dishes in the sink and junk mail. Bills. A computer and a TV. Old DVDs in the corner. Ari flipped through a few titles.

"Mostly, I stream now." Jonathan scratched the back of his head.

Everything was so—mundane. "This feels like home." Even more than their own apartment did. An unbidden, heady thought.

Every time Jonathan touched them, everything turned wondrous and dangerous, and this was no exception—a caress between the shoulders, meant to sooth. Ari turned to and pulled Jonathan into a kiss, one deep, full of exploration, and bent on subjection. Under Ari's palms, he trembled.

Such a simple thing. They pulled back. "You could kill me."

He stroked their cheek. "No, I can't," he whispered, painfully almost. "You're stronger than you know."

That's where this terror came from. Ari closed their eyes and leaned against him. Strong arms wrapped around them. All was crystal and light, like the selenite on their altar or the shimmer in Jonathan's scarf. He and this damn house fit Ari in a way nothing ever had. The cosmos looked back when Ari peered at Jonathan. *They* were the one who should be afraid.

And they *were*. So terrified that they could only move forward. "You gonna show me your bedroom?"

A chuckle. "Yes. Though the bed is far less...practical than yours."

"I'm sure I can find a way to tie you down." Ari let Jonathan's warmth and element flow into them. Pushed it back into Jonathan.

A sigh and another tremble. "I have no doubt. No doubt at all."

Weave me a spell.

Ari unwrapped themself from Jonathan. "What do you want?"

"Whatever you're willing to give. Or take."

That didn't help at all. "Let's see this bedroom of yours."

Jonathan led them upstairs, and yes, the bed was less practical for tying someone up, but Ari managed. In the end, Jonathan cried out their name like an invocation as Ari wove a very different kind of magic into him, one born of blood and sobs.

Afterward, Jonathan held Ari and murmured absently, as tears welled in Ari's eyes. "Tell me about stars."

Jonathan did, with words that made sense and ones that didn't, and then whispered truths in a language Ari didn't know. About loneliness and eternity. Falling to earth. The song of the universe that still echoed in Jonathan's ears. Ari shuddered and listened. Cold fire wrapped into their marrow, and *that* at least they understood. Jonathan was here, now. And so was Ari.

It had been two days since the ice rink. The moon hadn't even become full. Ari wanted whatever this was to last for the rest of their life, except their life would snuff out fast in the long exhale of Jonathan's.

They knew of no spell that would fix that.

5

JONATHAN'S BOOKSTORE REFLECTED HIM. The shop brimmed with the old and new, light and darkness, and held his sense of passion and cold fire. Ari touched the leather-clad spine of a tome and soaked in all that was Jonathan, just as they had the previous night and this morning.

The starlight. The eternity. The joy. "This shop is beautiful."

Jonathan's smile was everything. "Thank you. I'm glad you like it."

They stood close, like lovers, near a door marked STAFF in the back of the shop. Jonathan's employee, Lillian, was at the checkout counter with a customer. Murmured conversation was as soothing as the leather under Ari's fingertips and the bruise peeking from beneath Jonathan's coat collar. "Do you need to work today?"

He hesitated before answering. "I usually work on Sundays, to catch up on paperwork and help Lil out. But I don't have to."

Ari closed the distance, slid their hands inside his coat,

and pressed into the violet mark they'd left behind. Jonathan closed his eyes and exhaled. "I don't want to interrupt your life any more than I have."

"Please interrupt my life, Ari." He opened his eyes. "I have no desire to chase you away."

But there needed to be space. Ari'd always longed for both companionship and solitude. Spaces between to think and ponder. Right now, they didn't want to leave, but space could be opened here too. "I could read while you worked." They stroked his collarbone.

"That would be... It would be lovely to have you here."

So, after they stole a lingering kiss, Ari stayed. A quick perusal of the store, and they found an old action-adventure book to read. They settled into one of the comfortable chairs scattered around, and tucked their legs up, their long blue skirt keeping them warm from the occasional rush of cold air when the front door opened.

Jonathan flitted between the back room and the front counter, his occasional laugh a counterpoint to the general quiet of the store. Hours passed. Jonathan would stop by, and Ari would pull him down for a kiss and revel in the sweet taste of submission and sharp bite of starlight.

Some customers eyed Ari with curiosity—but not hostility—though they did overhear a murmured question and then Jonathan's clear response. "Oh, they're with me."

Yes, and no. Jonathan was with *them*, but that would undoubtedly be lost on most people. Ari glanced away from their book and stared unfocused at the shelves across from them. A thought twisted and swooped in the back of their mind—but they couldn't form the words to tease it out. It was all emotion and longing. Somehow, Jonathan was *theirs*. They didn't fucking care that it had only been three days.

Ari reached out and tugged on the strands of Jonathan's

energy swirling between them. A moment later he walked around a bookcase into the aisle, concern marring his expression. "Are you all right?"

No. "Yes." No. Ari closed the book, unfolded their legs, and stood. "No." They still hadn't processed all that had happened, what they'd learned, and all Jonathan had whispered to them last night.

Jonathan held out a hand, in offering. Ari took it, pulled him to them, and wrapped their arms around him. "You're overwhelming."

A huff of breath hit their ear. "You too, my witch."

Ari held him tighter. "You're not chasing me away, but I need to go home. Alone."

"I know," Jonathan murmured. "Space. Time. Both are needed to build a relationship."

Ari open a gap between them. "Jonathan—"

Bright fucking smile that took all of their willpower not to kiss away. "Not a romance. I know. But there are all kinds of relationships, Ari."

True and *true*. Didn't ease their desire to stay, nor the need to flee. Jonathan helped them into their coat and tugged at the starlight scarf around their neck. "This looks good on you."

"I still owe you a spell." They hadn't meant to say that.

"There's time, Ari. There's time."

Ari believed Jonathan then, but that wore off when they got to the T station. Their life was a blink, a moment to Jonathan. His was eternity in theirs.

Later, Ari watched shadows shift and move across the ceiling of their bedroom. Jonathan's scarf glowed softly on the chair they'd thrown it over, and the elements they could see and touch slithered through the room like forgotten memories.

Jonathan was *theirs*. That was the spell they'd been casting all this time. The one they'd begun at Samhain.

Weave me a spell.

"Did you know what you were asking for when you asked me that?"

The room didn't answer, but the scarf twinkled brighter.

6

ARI WAITED before setting their plan in motion. The moon became full, then waned, then waxed again, and Midwinter loomed—the darkest day, the longest night.

In between, Ari's life meshed with Jonathan's and his with theirs. Jonathan answered questions and pointed out the hidden mysteries of Pittsburgh. Their spells became stronger. Focused.

And they worked. Even Bess and Theo had accepted that Ari had found a balance—and that Jonathan hadn't burned the apartment down—not that they spent much time there. Many nights, Ari would find Jonathan waiting in the lobby of their office building. Sometimes, they'd go to dinner. Other times, they went ice skating. Most times, Ari fucked Jonathan. Or tied him up. Or both. But when they became so overwhelmed by Jonathan, when they'd taken too much, he'd hold Ari and whisper reassurances.

There was so *much* of Jonathan, of the light and darkness. Of submission, his need, his desire. All things Ari wanted to take and take and give back in spades.

They were human, though. Jonathan wasn't. The welts

and bruises and broken skin Ari left behind faded fast, *so* fast. Yet the impact lingered in Ari for much longer.

Still, Jonathan *fit* with Ari, so much so that Ari brought Jonathan to Thanksgiving dinner. Their circle-mate, Matty, upon meeting Jonathan, looked him up and down and rolled his eyes. "Of course someone like you would fall out of the sky for fricking Ari Zydik. They have all the luck." Then he'd sat down and included Jonathan in their circle. "You've got an altar or something, or do you just exist as a giant glowing thing?"

There'd been silence for a moment; then Jonathan had plopped himself on the floor next to Matty. "I'm, in fact, a giant glowing thing. But I also have an altar."

That was true. After the second night Ari'd spent at Jonathan's, they'd explored the house, with his blessing. In a small room full of art and books and plants stood an altar not too different from the one in their own room. "You ever afraid your candles will burn your books?"

"No." Jonathan had appeared behind them and wrapped his arms around Ari. Warm. Soothing, especially here. A candle had flamed to life on the altar. "We're alike, you and me. I can play with fire too."

"A magnifying glass and a sunny day."

He'd brushed his mouth along Ari's neck. "Something like that."

Ari had turned around and backed Jonathan against a wall, then set about harnessing his energy in an entirely different way.

MIDWINTER EVENING, Jonathan was waiting for them in the lobby of their office after work. He held out his arm as he so often did. "Shall we?"

Ari snorted, but took his arm anyway. As always. "It's Midwinter."

"Mmmm. A day for death, rebirth, and sacrifice." Jonathan's smile made Ari feel like tripping over the edge of a knife. "What does your heart want on this night?"

Ari exhaled breath like fire into the chilled night air. Possession. Domination. Someone who understood them. Held them. Let them be. "Let's go to your house." They were close to Gateway station.

They took the T to the familiar stop and walked the familiar blocks to Jonathan's home. Like always, Jonathan hung Ari's coat and scarf in the closet alongside his own, and like always, Ari climbed the stairs to the second floor. They stopped at the threshold of Jonathan's study and gazed at the altar.

Jonathan's energy wrapped around Ari before his arms did. They covered his hands with their own and leaned against him. "Do you have chalk and salt?"

They'd never *felt* Jonathan go still like he sometimes did, that inhuman moment. For an instant, he was as hard as a statue. Maybe his heart stopped beating. Then air rushed by their ear, and his weight slumped against theirs. "Yes, of course." Then words they'd heard on the first night. "Weave me a spell."

That fire—all the fire they'd collected—sparked in Ari, born of earth and what they'd taken again and again from Jonathan. They moved like flame too, spinning in Jonathan's arms, grappling him down until his hair was in their hands. He knelt at Ari's feet a moment later.

Shock, fight, then sweet surrender. The barest hint of a groan.

"I'll weave you a collar." The words poured from Ari like starlight and night—cold and eternal. "Keep you. Own you. Use you. Be with you."

Those beautiful eyes mirrored the fire Ari wove. Jonathan bent his body toward them. "Yes."

They pulled Jonathan's head back, exposing his throat. The sheer joy in his face nearly undid Ari. "Is that what you want? To be bound to me?"

"Please." His word was a promise.

Sparks danced along Ari's skin. They loosened their hold on Jonathan's hair. "I'm mortal." Ephemeral.

When Jonathan met their gaze, his eyes were nebulas. "You wouldn't be. Not after." He brushed his fingers against Ari's. "Take me. Keep me. Bind me, fire witch. I'll be by your side for as long as you wish."

This was a gift and a curse. One that they'd had been given that first night, part of a spell Ari'd been weaving since then. Terrible things flowed through Ari. Wonderful things too. "Why?"

Jonathan's brilliant smile flashed. "You saw me. Called me. You understand the spaces between." He paused. "And you *care*."

"I care," Ari echoed. They *did* care for Jonathan. Deeply. There was power there, such energy waiting to be held in their hands. The absolute joy of hearing Jonathan cry and beg and weep. Tasting his skin and blood. Thrusting into his pliant body. Trust lay in Ari too. The willingness to give Jonathan what he desired, what he *needed*. "You care too."

Jonathan's chuckle was a deep vibration Ari felt in their

bones. "Very much so. Finish weaving me into you, Ari Zydik. Claim me as your own."

They carded their fingers through Jonathan's silver hair. "Get chalk and salt, and a knife. Lose the clothes."

Jonathan's energy whipped around the room until Ari gathered it, calmed it, and drew him in. That came as naturally as breathing, taking what Jonathan gave. Controlling the power. As Ari tugged on Jonathan's hair again, realization cut through, shifting their life into singular clarity. "I've never been a fire witch. It's a fluke that I can manipulate fire."

Jonathan's sigh wasn't an answer, but the truth hung between them, as bright as Jonathan himself.

Ari spoke it into being. "I'm a *star* witch."

"Take me. Use me, Ari." Jonathan spoke softly. "I'll get you what you need."

They let go. "It'll be painful."

His smile glinted like a blade. "I know."

And it was, for both of them. Jonathan was Ari's altar; they were the sacrifice. Naked and glorious, they fought and fucked until Ari tamed Jonathan in a circle of chalk and salt. Took him and used him as he'd demanded, then wove them both together with blood, tears, and starlight. In the end, they lay tangled together on the hard floor of Jonathan's office, the copper smell of blood mixing with the scent of wax and sandalwood. Ari didn't need to open their eyes to know exactly where Jonathan was, how he looked, where tears dotted his face.

"I'm sorry you've been so lonely." Jonathan's sweet voice touched their soul.

Ari shifted and open their eyes, alone no more. "I wove you a spell. All this time, I wove *you*."

"You did. In every way I hoped you might."

"Have you always been this much of a manipulative bastard?" Ari pushed a bloodstained lock of hair away from Jonathan's eyes.

There was the grin they were so very fond of. "Yes."

Powerful. Bright. Strong. *Theirs.* "What now?"

"Now? You break your circle, my witch, and we take a shower. After that? The future is yours."

"Ours," they said.

"This isn't a romance, Ari," he murmured.

No, it wasn't. But Jonathan was theirs, and they were his, so it didn't really matter. They reached out with their foot and broke the circle.

AFTERWORD

As with my other books set in Pittsburgh, this one contains some homages to the city that I love. Many of the locations described in this book exist, including the rink that pops up each winter in PPG Plaza and the Point State Park fountain. I do hope you enjoy the little glimpse of Pittsburgh. It's a magical place.

Astute readers who have also read my novel *Close Quarter* may notice that the world-building here is similar. That's intentional. While there's no crossover with that novel, the universe is the same.

ALSO BY ANNA ZABO

Close Quarter

Close Quarter

Slow Waltz (a Close Quarter short story)

Takeover

Takeover

Just Business

Due Diligence

Daily Grind

Twisted Wishes

Syncopation

Counterpoint

Reverb

Standalone Works

CTRL Me

Outside the Lines

Weave the Dark, Weave the Light

Cinnamon Roll

ABOUT THE AUTHOR

Anna Zabo writes contemporary and paranormal romance for all colors of the rainbow. They live and work in Pittsburgh, Pennsylvania, which isn't nearly as boring as most people think.

They can be easily plied with coffee or a chance to see the Pittsburgh Penguins.

Anna has an MFA in Writing Popular Fiction from Seton Hill University, where they fell in with a roving band of romance writers and never looked back. They also have a BA in Creative Writing from Carnegie Mellon University.

Anna uses they/them pronouns and prefers Mx. Zabo as an honorific. They can be found online at annazabo.com.

twitter.com/amergina

instagram.com/amergina

bookbub.com/authors/anna-zabo

amazon.com/Anna-Zabo/e/B00A7LA6OC